POP-POP AIRPLANE
HOW DO YOU FLY?

Dan Pegram

ILLUSTRATED BY Mike Richardson

BROWN BOOKS KIDS

Pop-Pop Airplane, How Do You Fly?

Brown Books Kids
16250 Knoll Trail Drive, Suite 205
Dallas, Texas 75248
www.BrownBooksKids.com
(972) 381-0009

A New Era in Publishing®

Publisher's Cataloging-In-Publication Data

Names: Pegram, Dan, 1953- author. | Richardson, Mike, 1982- illustrator.
Title: Pop Pop Airplane, how do you fly? / Dan Pegram ; illustrated by Mike Richardson.
Other Titles: Pop-Pop Airplane, how do you fly?
Description: Dallas, Texas : Brown Books Kids, [2019] | Interest age level: 003-006. | Summary: "Ever wonder how airplanes fly in the sky? Pop-Pop Airplane is here to teach you a little something about them, from wings to engine and the parts in between. See how much you can learn from Pop-Pop Airplane!"—Provided by publisher.
Identifiers: ISBN 9781612543208
Subjects: LCSH: Airplanes—Design and construction—Juvenile literature. | Flight—Juvenile literature. | CYAC: Airplanes--Design and construction. | Flight.
Classification: LCC TL547 .P44 2019 | DDC 629.13334 [E]—dc23

ISBN 978-1-61254-320-8
LCCN 2019936820

Printed in China
10 9 8 7 6 5 4 3 2 1

For more information or to contact the author, please go to
www.PopPopAirplane.com.

Dedication

*I'd like to dedicate this book to our grandchildren
Bailey and Charlotte, who first called me Pop-Pop,
and to Kamden, who, knowing I was an airline pilot,
would point to all airplanes in the sky and say,
"Pop-Pop airplane."*

Acknowledgments

I would like to thank my wife, Suzanne, who endured forty-plus years of aviation and inspired me to write this book. I'd also like to thank my daughter-in-law, Katy, for her hours of research, which led me to discover my wonderful publishers at Brown Books. Lastly, I'd like to say a very special thank you to Mike Richardson, an incredibly talented artist and illustrator, who captured my vision and brought this book to life.

How do you soar so high in the sky?"

I have so much I want to share with you.

Gather around, children, and take a chair

while I explain how I take to the air.

My big rubber tires go round and round.

That's how I move around on the ground.

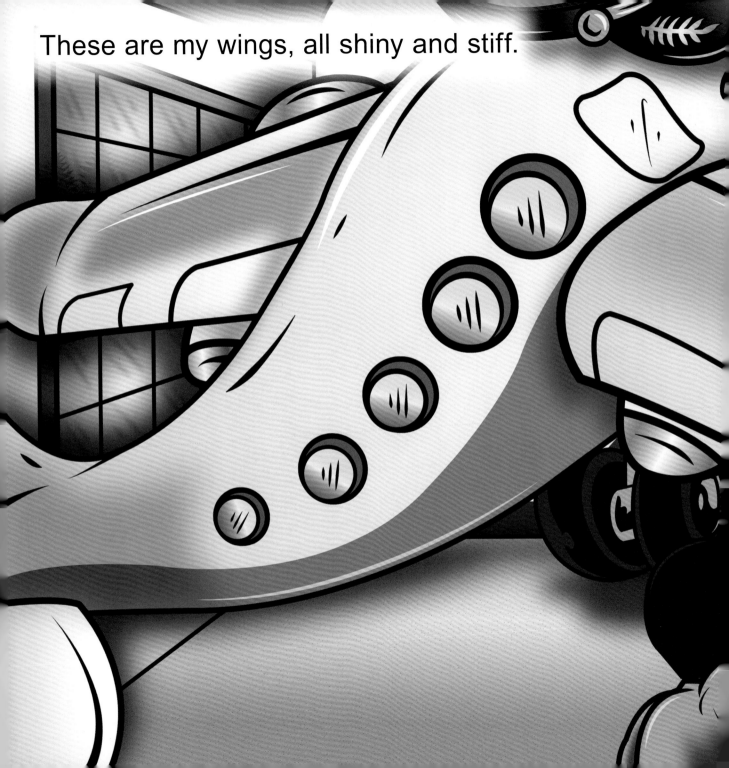

These are my wings, all shiny and stiff.

My rudder keeps me flying in a straight line,

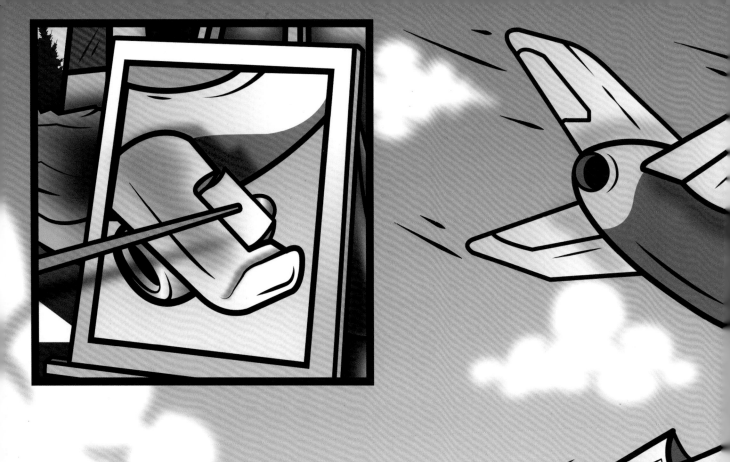

My ailerons help me while I'm in flight

to gently turn both left and right.

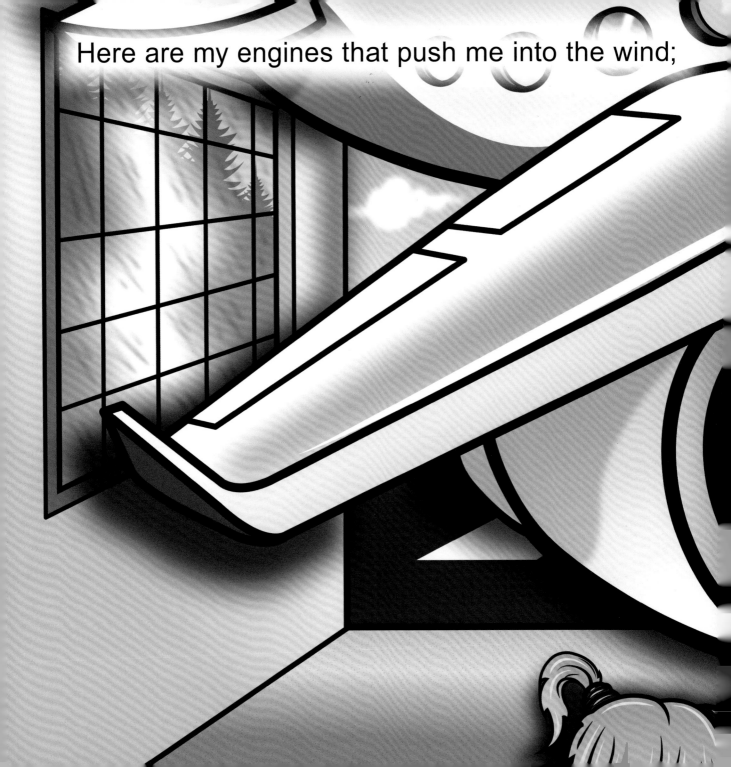

Here are my engines that push me into the wind;

The wind across my wings is what really makes me go, so I can soar high above all the houses below.

Well, my friends, it's time for my flight.
The sky is blue, and the winds are light.

So when you and your family decide to travel by air,
I'll be waiting at the airport to take you there.

"How the ground rumbles as your big engines roar!
We love you, Pop-Pop Airplane, and how high you soar."

aBOUT THe aUTHOR

Dan Pegram is a retired United States Air Force lieutenant colonel and command pilot who flew the KC-135 aerial refueling aircraft. After his retirement from the US Air Force, Dan worked at Southwest Airlines, where he served as a Boeing 737 captain and chairman of the airline union's professional standards committee.

Dan Pegram is now the president of Contrail Creations LLC, which is dedicated to children's education, literacy, and marketing.

Dan resides in Crowley, Texas, with his wife, Suzanne. They are the proud parents of daughter Leslie and sons Brian and Kevin. They have three grand-children, Bailey, Charlotte, and Kamden.

aBOUT THe ILLUSTRaTOR

Mike Richardson is a multidisciplinary visual artist based out of North Carolina. Art became Mike's driving force early on when he discovered his ability to leave a mark on the world around him using a simple box of crayons. From that moment forward, everything within reach became a canvas for his artistic expression. After receiving encouragement through middle and high school from peers and teachers, he decided to pursue art as a career.

In 2005, Mike earned a BFA in painting and printmaking from Appalachian State University and received an associate's degree in graphic design and illustration from Guilford Technical Community College in 2010. Currently, Mike is the creative force behind Rebel Soul Studio, where he uses his unique illustration style to create poster prints, apparel, stickers, skateboards, hand-painted custom shoes, and original paintings.

Mike lives in Raleigh, North Carolina, with his wife, Jennilee, and their two amazing children, Olivia and Hendrix.